N. Gould

THE DUTCH TILES

The Dutch Tiles

Story by
PAMELA STAPLETON

Pictures by
EVADNE ROWAN

FREDERICK WARNE & CO. LTD : London

FREDERICK WARNE & CO. INC : New York

LIBRARY OF CONGRESS CATALOG
CARD NO. 69-20110

FULL BOUND EDITION 7232 1002 0
LIBRARY STYLE EDITION 7232 1031 4

7232 1002 0

Printed in Great Britain by
Fleming & Humphreys (Baylis) Ltd
Leicester

JONATHAN loved the Dutch tiles around the fireplace in his room. They were a lovely soft blue colour, like his dressing-gown. All of them were different, but on each one there was a little boat with a blue sail.

At night when he was tucked up in bed, Jonathan would say, 'Please Mummy, tell me the story of the Little Boat.' And she would sit on the edge of his bed and begin . . .

There was once a Little Boat with a blue sail that lived on a lake in the middle of a dark, dark wood. There were so many trees around the lake that the wind never blew hard there, and so the Little Boat could never sail very fast. Even the fish went faster than he did, and they used to laugh at him as they swam by. This made the Little Boat sad.

'What shall I do?' he asked the Gloomy Castle by the side of the lake. But the Castle only closed his eyes and pretended not to hear.

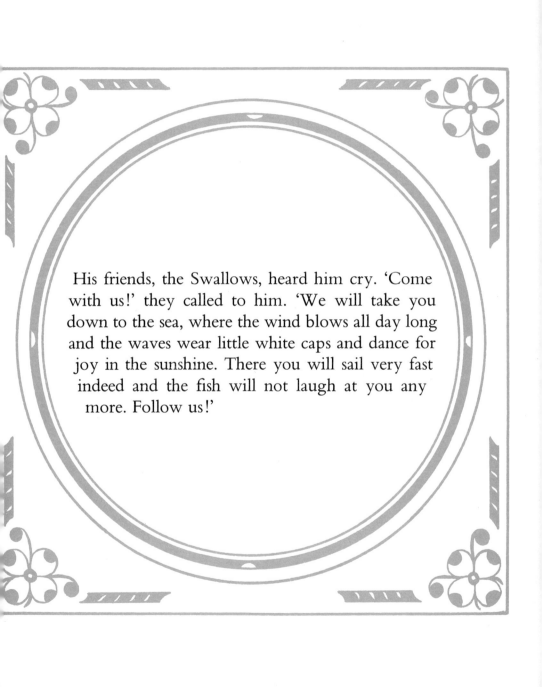

His friends, the Swallows, heard him cry. 'Come with us!' they called to him. 'We will take you down to the sea, where the wind blows all day long and the waves wear little white caps and dance for joy in the sunshine. There you will sail very fast indeed and the fish will not laugh at you any more. Follow us!'

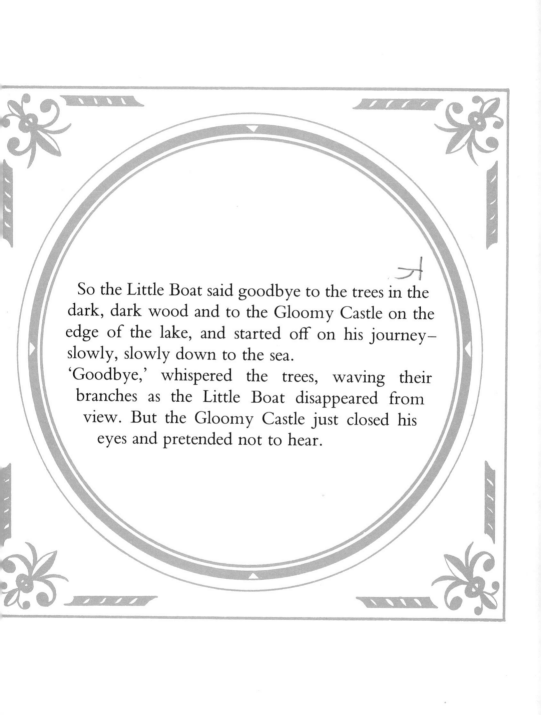

So the Little Boat said goodbye to the trees in the
dark, dark wood and to the Gloomy Castle on the
edge of the lake, and started off on his journey—
slowly, slowly down to the sea.

'Goodbye,' whispered the trees, waving their
branches as the Little Boat disappeared from
view. But the Gloomy Castle just closed his
eyes and pretended not to hear.

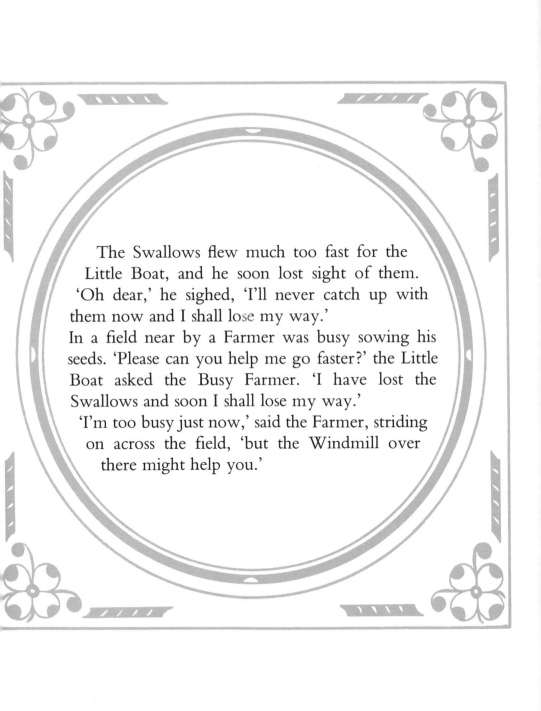

The Swallows flew much too fast for the
Little Boat, and he soon lost sight of them.
'Oh dear,' he sighed, 'I'll never catch up with
them now and I shall lose my way.'
In a field near by a Farmer was busy sowing his
seeds. 'Please can you help me go faster?' the Little
Boat asked the Busy Farmer. 'I have lost the
Swallows and soon I shall lose my way.'
  'I'm too busy just now,' said the Farmer, striding
    on across the field, 'but the Windmill over
        there might help you.'

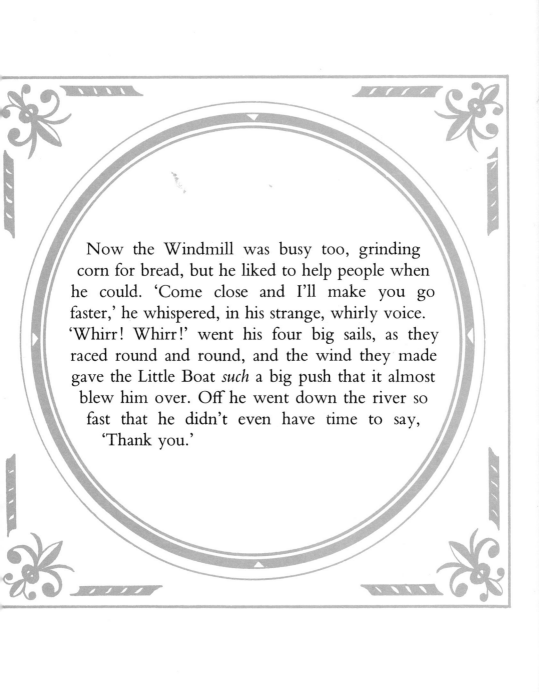

Now the Windmill was busy too, grinding corn for bread, but he liked to help people when he could. 'Come close and I'll make you go faster,' he whispered, in his strange, whirly voice. 'Whirr! Whirr!' went his four big sails, as they raced round and round, and the wind they made gave the Little Boat *such* a big push that it almost blew him over. Off he went down the river so fast that he didn't even have time to say, 'Thank you.'

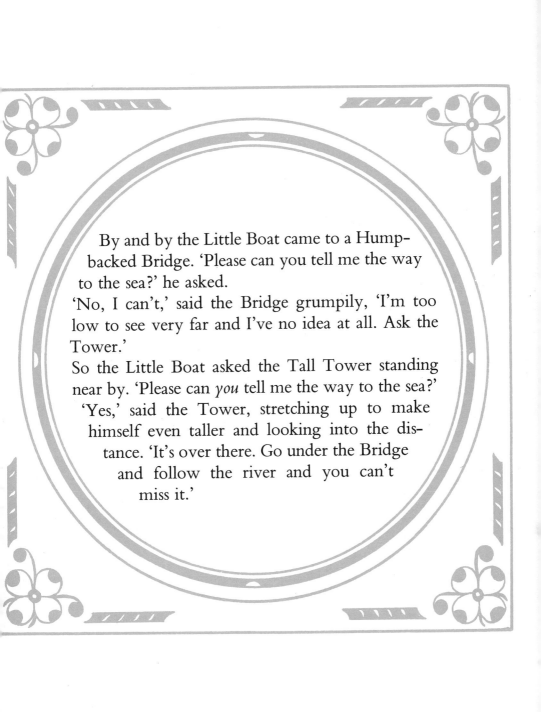

By and by the Little Boat came to a Hump-backed Bridge. 'Please can you tell me the way to the sea?' he asked.

'No, I can't,' said the Bridge grumpily, 'I'm too low to see very far and I've no idea at all. Ask the Tower.'

So the Little Boat asked the Tall Tower standing near by. 'Please can *you* tell me the way to the sea?'

'Yes,' said the Tower, stretching up to make himself even taller and looking into the distance. 'It's over there. Go under the Bridge and follow the river and you can't miss it.'

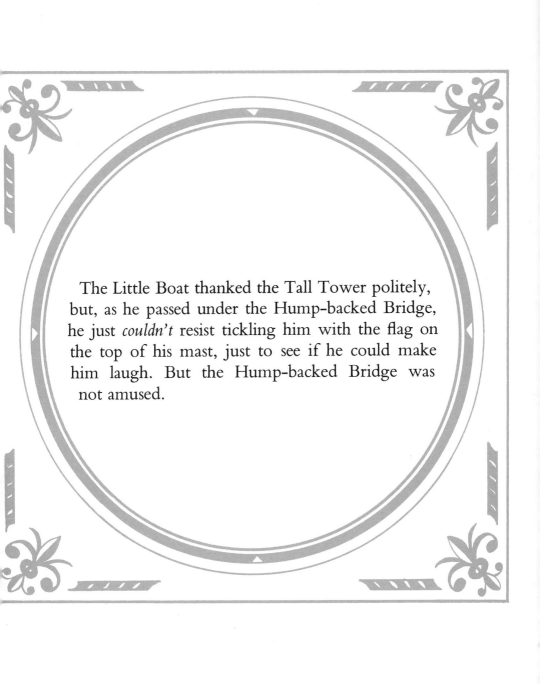

The Little Boat thanked the Tall Tower politely, but, as he passed under the Hump-backed Bridge, he just *couldn't* resist tickling him with the flag on the top of his mast, just to see if he could make him laugh. But the Hump-backed Bridge was not amused.

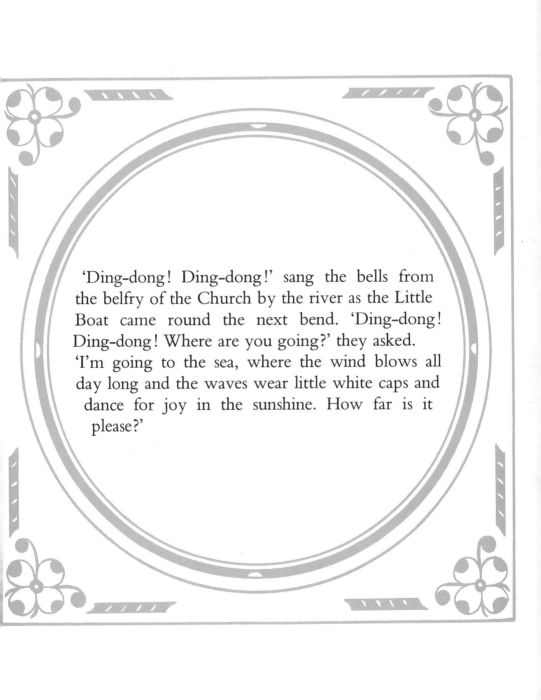

'Ding-dong! Ding-dong!' sang the bells from the belfry of the Church by the river as the Little Boat came round the next bend. 'Ding-dong! Ding-dong! Where are you going?' they asked. 'I'm going to the sea, where the wind blows all day long and the waves wear little white caps and dance for joy in the sunshine. How far is it please?'

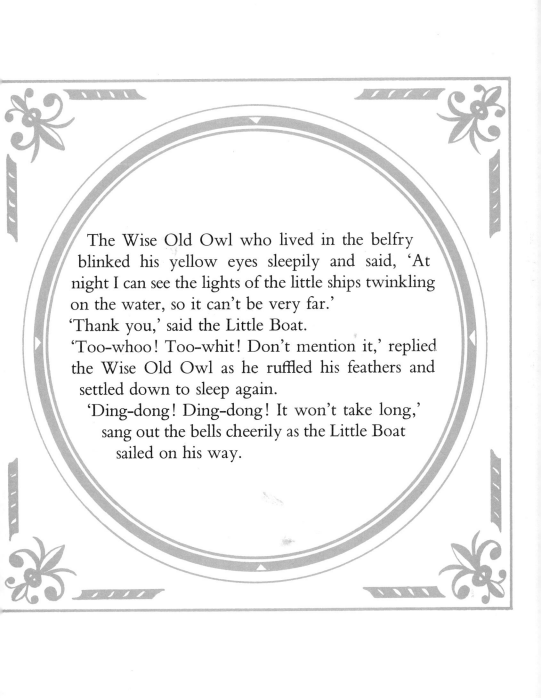

The Wise Old Owl who lived in the belfry blinked his yellow eyes sleepily and said, 'At night I can see the lights of the little ships twinkling on the water, so it can't be very far.'

'Thank you,' said the Little Boat.

'Too-whoo! Too-whit! Don't mention it,' replied the Wise Old Owl as he ruffled his feathers and settled down to sleep again.

'Ding-dong! Ding-dong! It won't take long,' sang out the bells cheerily as the Little Boat sailed on his way.

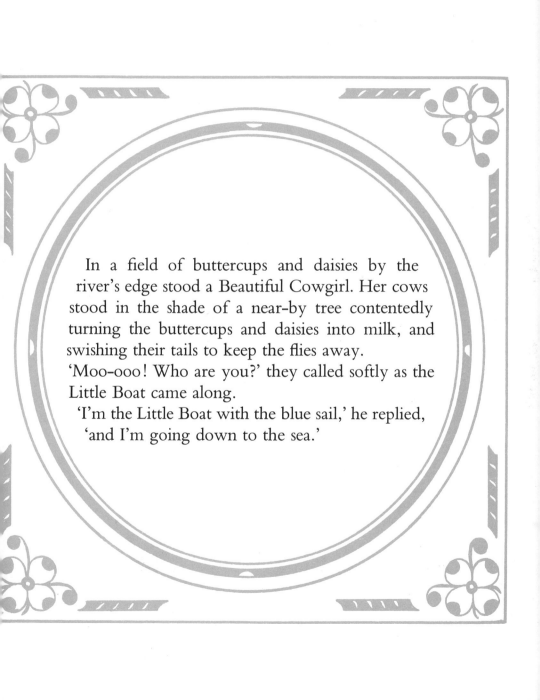

In a field of buttercups and daisies by the river's edge stood a Beautiful Cowgirl. Her cows stood in the shade of a near-by tree contentedly turning the buttercups and daisies into milk, and swishing their tails to keep the flies away.
'Moo-ooo! Who are you?' they called softly as the Little Boat came along.
'I'm the Little Boat with the blue sail,' he replied, 'and I'm going down to the sea.'

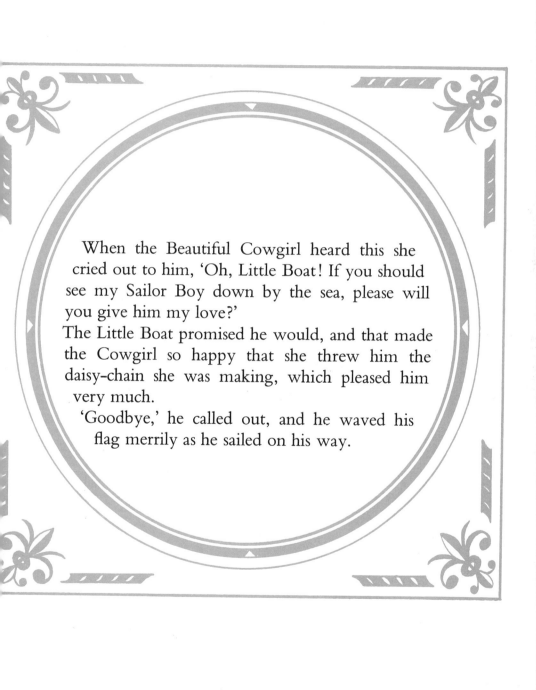

When the Beautiful Cowgirl heard this she cried out to him, 'Oh, Little Boat! If you should see my Sailor Boy down by the sea, please will you give him my love?'

The Little Boat promised he would, and that made the Cowgirl so happy that she threw him the daisy-chain she was making, which pleased him very much.

'Goodbye,' he called out, and he waved his flag merrily as he sailed on his way.

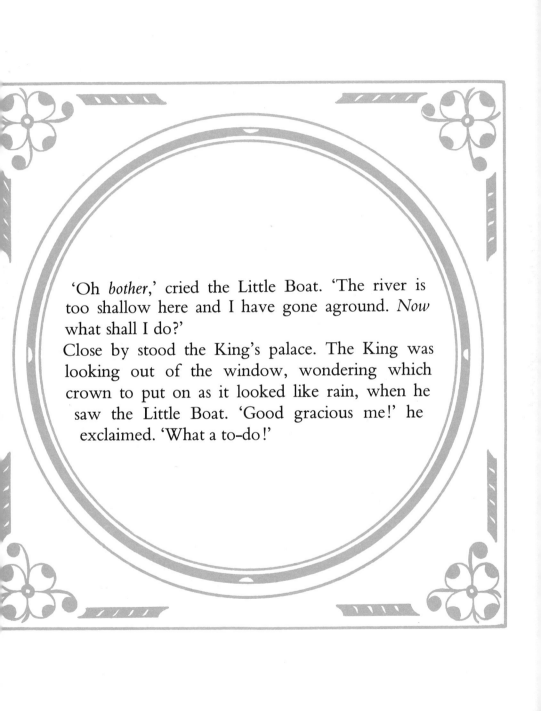

'Oh *bother*,' cried the Little Boat. 'The river is too shallow here and I have gone aground. *Now* what shall I do?'

Close by stood the King's palace. The King was looking out of the window, wondering which crown to put on as it looked like rain, when he saw the Little Boat. 'Good gracious me!' he exclaimed. 'What a to-do!'

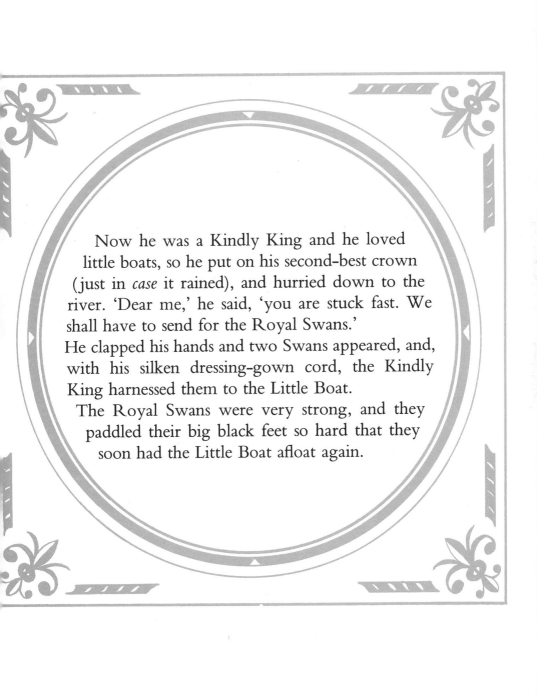

Now he was a Kindly King and he loved
little boats, so he put on his second-best crown
(just in *case* it rained), and hurried down to the
river. 'Dear me,' he said, 'you are stuck fast. We
shall have to send for the Royal Swans.'
He clapped his hands and two Swans appeared, and,
with his silken dressing-gown cord, the Kindly
King harnessed them to the Little Boat.
The Royal Swans were very strong, and they
paddled their big black feet so hard that they
soon had the Little Boat afloat again.

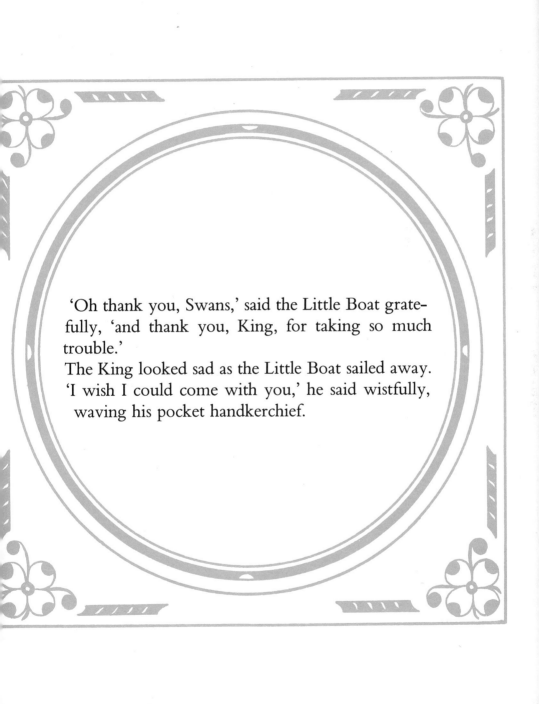

'Oh thank you, Swans,' said the Little Boat grate-
fully, 'and thank you, King, for taking so much
trouble.'
The King looked sad as the Little Boat sailed away.
'I wish I could come with you,' he said wistfully,
waving his pocket handkerchief.

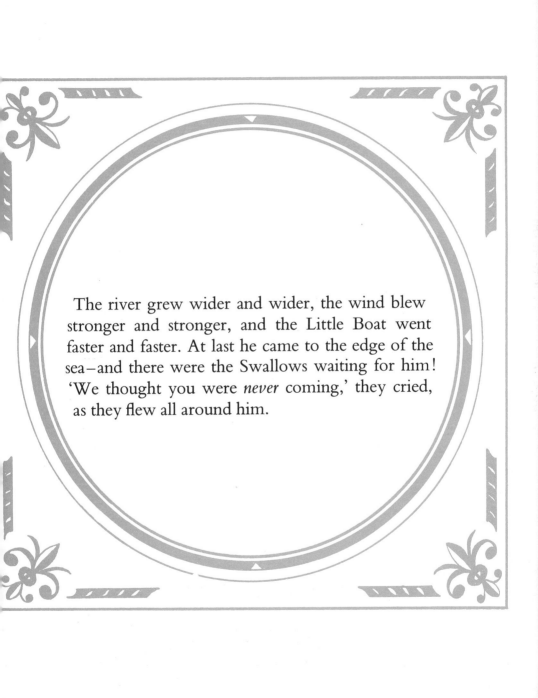

The river grew wider and wider, the wind blew stronger and stronger, and the Little Boat went faster and faster. At last he came to the edge of the sea—and there were the Swallows waiting for him! 'We thought you were *never* coming,' they cried, as they flew all around him.

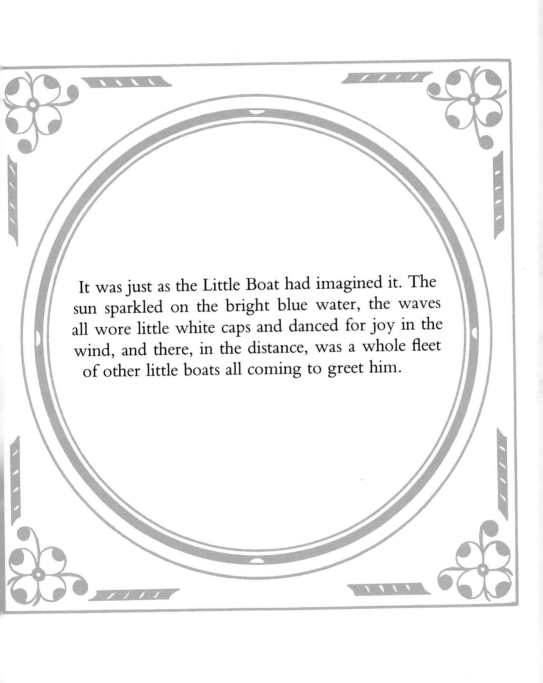

It was just as the Little Boat had imagined it. The sun sparkled on the bright blue water, the waves all wore little white caps and danced for joy in the wind, and there, in the distance, was a whole fleet of other little boats all coming to greet him.

The Little Boat was tired, but very, very happy.
He puffed out his blue sail in the beautiful wind and
sailed away into the sunset to meet them.

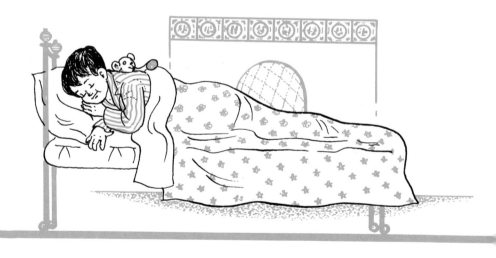